Clue Jr. ™

festorius

The Case of the Barking Dog

Look for these Clue™ Jr. books!

The Case of the Barking Dog

Book created by Parker C. Hinter

Written by Della Rowland

Illustrated by Diamond Studio

Based on characters from the Parker Brothers game

A Creative Media Applications Production

SCHOLASTIC INC.
New York Toronto London Auckland Sydney

ISBN 0-590-13786-7

Copyright © 1997 by Hasbro, Inc. All rights reserved. Published by Scholastic Inc., by arrangement with Parker Brothers, a division of Hasbro, Inc. CLUE ® is a registered trademark of Hasbro, Inc. for its detective game equipment.

12 11 10 9 8 7 6 5   8 9/9 0 1 2/0

Printed in the U.S.A.   40

First Scholastic printing, October 1997

Contents

The Case of the Tree House Visitor

"**S**amantha! Let's go!" Greta Green yelled from outside Samantha Scarlet's house. Samantha poked her head out of her upstairs bedroom window. Standing in the front yard below were Greta, Peter, and Mortimer. "Hi, guys!" she said, waving to them.

"Hurry, Samantha!" shouted Greta. "If you don't come now, I'm going to be late and Coach won't let me start!" The Clue Club kids were going to Greta's soccer game that afternoon. As usual, they were waiting for Samantha, who was always late.

"I'm coming," Samantha yelled down. "I'm just getting off the phone."

It was a beautiful autumn day. The weather was crisp and the turning leaves were beginning to fall. Samantha grabbed her jacket and dashed out her front door. Turning, she locked the door behind her. Then she jumped off the porch and ran across the yard to the others. "Here I am," she called.

"Who were you talking to?" asked Peter as they began walking.

"Veronica Verdant," Samantha answered. "She borrowed my new video of *The Mystery of Mouse Manor* and I was telling her to bring it back today."

"Wow! You have that movie?" exclaimed Mortimer. "Can we watch it after the game?"

"I'd love to!" said Samantha. "I got the movie two weeks ago and I haven't seen it yet."

"So why'd you lend it to Veronica?" said Mortimer, shaking his head. "She never gives anything back."

"Yeah, I know," sighed Samantha. "She was supposed to return it last weekend, but she always has some excuse. Nobody's

home at my house today, but I didn't want to give her another excuse, so I told her just to leave it in my tree house."

"Good luck," said Greta. "You'll need it to get the movie back."

The kids made it to Greta's game just in time. As Peter, Mortimer, and Samantha were looking for a place to sit, Samantha spotted Veronica in the bleachers. "Hey! Veronica!" she called out. "Don't forget my movie!"

"I already delivered it," Veronica shouted back.

"In the tree house, right?" Samantha asked.

"Yep, just like you told me," said Veronica. "It was easy. I just climbed up the ladder and left it inside."

"Great," Samantha said, relieved. She turned to her friends. "Whew! I was afraid I'd never get to see my own movie."

After the game, the kids went back to Samantha's. When they reached her house, they ran straight to the backyard to get the video. "I can't wait to see this movie," said Samantha climbing up into the tree house.

"Isn't this new?" said Mortimer, pointing to the tree house ladder.

"It looks like it," said Peter.

"You got the movie?" Greta shouted up to Samantha.

"No," Samantha called down to the others. "It's not here."

"I told you," said Greta. "You'll never get your movie back."

Samantha climbed back down and the kids went to the back door. To Samantha's surprise, the door was open. Inside, her father stood at the kitchen counter, making a sandwich.

"Hi, Dad. When did you get home?" asked Samantha.

"Before you left for the game," Mr. Scarlet replied. "The meeting at the bank was canceled. I started to tell you I was here, but you were on the phone. Then you left while I was changing clothes."

"Did you see anyone come to the house?" asked Samantha.

"No," Mr. Scarlet answered. "But I've been down in my workshop all day. I decided to take care of some things that needed fixing around the house."

"Have you been sawing downstairs?" Samantha asked, pointing to his dusty overalls.

"Yes," he said. "I fixed the ladder for your tree house. In fact, I just finished it a little while ago—right before you got home."

"I thought so." Samantha laughed. "You're covered with sawdust."

"Oh, dear," her father said, frowning. "I'd better change before I get sawdust all over everything. Your mother will kill me!" He went quickly up the stairs.

"I'm going to call Veronica," said Samantha, heading to her room. In a few minutes she returned to the kitchen.

"Veronica says she left the video in the tree house," she told the others. "She says someone must have climbed up and taken it."

"She's a liar!" exclaimed Greta.

"Maybe," said Samantha. "She said it wasn't her fault the movie was gone because I told her to put it in the tree house, where it was easy for someone else to find."

"Oh brother!" said Peter.

"That's not all!" said Samantha. "Veronica said it wasn't her fault if people in my neighborhood steal!"

"Can you believe it?" said Greta.

"Yeah, but now what?" said Samantha. "There's no way to prove she didn't return my movie."

"But who else would have taken it?" said Greta.

"Well, someone at the soccer game could have heard Veronica telling you she put the video in the tree house," Peter pointed out.

"That's right!" said Samantha. "That means we really can't prove anything!"

"No, wait!" said Mortimer. "I think I can

prove that Veronica never brought the movie over."

How can Mortimer prove Veronica is lying?

SOLUTION
The Case of the Tree House Visitor

"She couldn't have left it in the tree house before the soccer game," said Mortimer. "She couldn't get into the tree house."

"Why not?" asked Samantha.

"Because there wasn't any ladder," said Mortimer. "Your dad fixed the ladder this afternoon, while we were at the soccer game, right? He took the ladder down to fix it."

"That's right," exclaimed Peter. "I noticed the ladder was gone when we were waiting for Samantha before the soccer game."

"So the ladder was gone until just a little while ago," said Greta. "Then there's no way Veronica could have gotten into the tree house."

"Right," agreed Mortimer. "But she didn't know the ladder was down."

"So she lied about even coming over," said Samantha. "There's my proof — the ladder."

"Yep," laughed Peter. "Without the ladder Veronica doesn't have a leg to stand on."

2

The Case of the Disappearing Brownies

"**W**ow!" exclaimed Mortimer. He and the other Clue Club kids were standing on the back porch of Greta's house looking at her backyard. It was covered with a thick carpet of yellow and red leaves that had fallen off the trees.

Mortimer whistled. "I thought there were a lot of leaves in the front," he said. "But there are even more back here."

"Yes, it's a big job, " said Mrs. Green. "I really appreciate your help."

"We're just lucky it's not a windy day," said Samantha. "My dad and I raked last weekend, right after that big storm. As soon as we got the leaves into a pile, the wind blew them all over the yard again."

"Well, there's no wind today," said Greta,

holding up one of her fingers. "The air is perfectly still."

"I liked the air in the kitchen better," Mortimer said. "Mrs. Green, there are brownies in the oven, right?"

"Yes," said Mrs. Green. She smiled at Mortimer. "They'll be cool enough to cut by the time you're finished raking."

"Great!" exclaimed Mortimer. "I love brownies."

Mrs. Green laughed. "I know, Mortimer," she said. "And pizza, too. That's why I've ordered *two* pies. They'll be delivered here in an hour."

The kids raked up all the leaves out front and piled them along the street curb. Then they started on the backyard. Soon they had several large piles of leaves ready to cart to the front curb.

"The pizza is here!" Mrs. Green called out to the kids. "Come eat it while it's hot. You can finish raking the backyard after lunch."

"Yeesss!" cried Mortimer. "I'm starving." He and the kids ran into the house to wash up.

After lunch, the kids went back to raking. When they were nearly finished, Mrs. Green came out with a plate of brownies and some napkins. She set the plate and napkins on the picnic table.

"I thought you'd like to sit in this nice clean backyard to have your brownies," she said. "That way you can admire all your hard work."

"Mmmm," said Mortimer. "I don't care where we eat them, as long as we have milk, too."

"Stop drooling and finish raking, Mortimer," said Peter. "The quicker we finish, the quicker we can eat the brownies."

"Yeah," said Samantha. "Besides, the brownies won't run away."

After the kids finished piling the leaves at the curb, they raced to the garage to put their rakes away. Then they trooped inside, washed their hands, grabbed glasses of milk, and headed back to the picnic table.

As they turned the corner of the house, they saw Greta's next-door neighbor, Charlie Charcoal, walking out the back fence gate.

"Hey, Charlie!" Greta called out. He turned around and waved.

"Hi," he said. "I just came over to see if you were home, but no one answered my knock."

"I guess we didn't hear you because we were washing up," said Greta. "Want a brownie?"

"Sure," said Charlie.

"Well, you'd better hurry," said Mortimer. "Because in about two minutes they'll all be gone." He looked over at the table, but the plate was empty.

"Whoa!" cried Greta. "They're already gone!"

"Charlie!" Mortimer yelled out. "What did you do with the brownies?"

"What brownies?" said Charlie.

"There was a whole plate of brownies on the table five minutes ago," Mortimer said. "They're gone. Did you just eat them?"

"How could I do that?" said Charlie. "I couldn't eat a plate of brownies that fast."

"Well, they couldn't just disappear," said Greta.

"What about your pockets?" said Samantha.

"Nothing up my sleeves, nothing in my pockets," said Charlie. He took off his jacket and turned his pants pockets wrong side out.

"You're not a magician, Charlie, but I think you made the brownies disappear," said Peter.

"But I don't have them!" cried Charlie.

"That's because we came outside before you could get away with them," said Peter.

"So where are they?" asked Charlie.

"Right where you put them," said Peter. "I'll show you."

How does Peter know Charlie hid the brownies? Where are they?

SOLUTION
The Case of the Disappearing Brownies

"Okay, Mr. Detective," said Charlie. "Where are the brownies?"

"Where the wind is blowing," said Peter.

"But there's no wind today," said Saman-tha.

Peter pointed toward a corner of the backyard. Everyone looked in that direction. Suddenly Mortimer ran over to the tire swing, which was moving back and forth.

"Here's what the wind is blowing," Mortimer said. He pulled a napkin full of brownies from the inside of the tire. "And here's where the brownies disappeared to."

"I get it," said Samantha. "There's no wind today. So how could the tire swing be moving?"

"Unless someone moved it," said Greta.

"Someone hiding something inside it, maybe?"

"Okay," admitted Charlie. "I saw the brownies from my window. I almost made it out the gate with them but I heard you guys coming back. So I stuck them in the tire."

"Well, I'm not a magician, either," said Mortimer with a grin. "But I'm going to make these brownies disappear again — into my mouth!"

3

The Case of the Birthday Party Clue

"Happy birthday, Peter!" yelled Mortimer, Greta, and Samantha when Peter opened his front door.

"Thanks, guys," Peter said, beaming. "Come on in. You're early. The party doesn't start until noon."

"We didn't want to miss anything," said Greta.

"What kind of cake did your mom make?" asked Mortimer.

"Chocolate Fudge Supreme," said Peter.

"Mmmm," said Mortimer. "My favorite."

"Here, Peter," said Samantha, handing Peter a box with a huge bow on it.

"Oh, great!" said Peter, shaking the box. "What is it?"

"Oh, you'll find out when you unwrap it," replied Samantha.

"Here's mine," said Greta, handing Peter a box.

"I have a present, too," said Mortimer. He brought a package from behind his back.

"Hey!" said Peter. "Thanks!"

Peter led everyone into the dining room. The room was decorated with ribbons and a banner that read, IT'S PETER'S BIRTHDAY! Peter put the presents on a small side table. "I was just going to bring the snacks from the kitchen," he told them. "Come carry something in."

"Sure," said Mortimer.

"Don't let Mortimer carry any food!" exclaimed Samantha. "Only half of it will get to the table."

The kids helped get everything set up for the party. But by 12:30, no one else had arrived. Peter was getting very upset. "How come no one is coming to my party?" he said. "Is everyone mad at me?"

"Don't be silly," said Mortimer. "Let's call them up and find out what happened."

The kids began calling the names on Peter's guest list. It turned out no one knew about the party. However, most of the kids could come anyway, so the Plums pushed the time for the party back to two o'clock.

"This is a mystery," said Peter. "I wonder why everyone forgot my party except you."

"Maybe you forgot to tell them," said Samantha.

"No. I mailed out invitations," Peter said.

"I guess we should feel special since you gave us ours at school," said Mortimer, pulling his invitation out of his back pocket.

"I like the Puzzle Pals invitations," said Samantha. "And the matching envelopes with magnifying glasses on them. They're great!"

"Yeah, 'Puzzle Pals' is my favorite TV show now," said Peter. "I love all the mysteries the kids solve."

"Me too," agreed Greta. "You know, we could solve those mysteries."

"Here's a mystery we could work on," said Mortimer. "What does Peter have planned for everyone to do at his party?"

"Yeah!" exclaimed Samantha. "Your invitation says to get ready for a mystery game. What is it?"

"Can't tell you," said Peter, smiling. "You'll have to figure it out. Or at least wait until everyone else gets here."

"Come on," said Mortimer. "Give us a clue, Peter."

"Okay," said Peter. "It's finding something."

"A scavenger hunt?" said Greta.

"Sort of," said Peter. "Each team gets a list of things to find. But the things are in a kind of code. First you have to figure out what they are before you can go find them. Cool, huh?"

"Yeah!" said Samantha. "So what time is it? How long before the rest of the kids get here?"

"Another twenty minutes," said Mortimer, looking at his watch.

Peter's mother came from the kitchen. "Peter, I can't believe this," she said. "I don't have candles for your cake. And now I've got to run over to the store and pick some up." She shook her head. "I know where you get your forgetfulness, Peter. From me!" She laughed. "It's a good thing everybody's coming late."

"Wait, Mom, we'll go get the candles," Peter told her.

"Sure, Mrs. Plum," said Greta. "We need something to keep us busy until the party starts."

"Oh, thanks, kids," Mrs. Plum said. "If you're sure you don't mind, that would be great."

"No problem," said Samantha as the kids ran to the closet for their jackets.

"Peter, you'd better wear your quilted jacket," his mother said. "It's chilly today."

"Oh, Mom," sighed Peter. "I hate that jacket."

"But you loved it when we bought it," his mother said. "Don't worry, sweetheart — one more year and it will be too small."

"I wish I could grow a foot in one day just so I wouldn't have to wear that stupid jacket," muttered Peter.

"I like it," said Mortimer.

"Great!" said Peter. "Here, Mortimer, you wear it. I'll wear yours." He handed Mortimer the quilted jacket.

"Hey! Okay!" exclaimed Mortimer, trading his jacket for Peter's.

As the kids headed for the door Peter perked up. "By the time we get back everyone will be here," he said. "Then we can play the mystery game."

"Hmm," said Greta. "I think I've already solved the first mystery of the day."

"What mystery?" asked Samantha.

"The mystery of why no one showed up for your party," said Greta.

"Why didn't they come?" asked Mortimer.

"Because they didn't know about it,"

said Greta. "You forgot to let them know, Peter."

How does Greta know Peter forgot to tell his guests about his birthday party?

SOLUTION
The Case of the Birthday Party Clue

"I forgot?" said Peter. "How do you know?"

"The clue is in your jacket pocket," said Greta, pointing to Peter's jacket, which Mortimer was wearing.

Everyone looked at the jacket. Slowly Peter pulled out his party invitations.

"Oops," he said, blushing. "I guess I forgot to mail these."

"You must have worn this jacket when you went to mail the invitations," said Samantha.

"Yeah," said Peter. "And I guess I haven't worn it since then. I try never to wear it."

"You forgot you put the invitations in the pocket," said Mortimer.

"You probably forgot where you were

going before you even got to the mailbox,"
said Greta, shaking her head.

"The only thing you didn't forget was
your birthday," laughed Samantha.

The Case of the Chess Caper

"*Brrriiinnng!*" rang the dismissal bell at school on Friday. The Clue Club kids met on the school grounds to walk home together. On the way, Mortimer reminded them of the garage sale his parents were having the next afternoon.

"My parents decided to get rid of some of their junk," Mortimer explained. "So they're having a garage sale before it gets too cold. I decided to set up my own table, too. I've got some things I don't want anymore."

"You do?" said Samantha. "I thought you never wanted to get rid of anything."

"Well, I do now," Mortimer replied. "Hey, do you guys want to bring anything to sell?"

"Yeah," said Peter. "Is it okay if the stuff isn't in perfect shape?"

"Sure," said Mortimer. "You just won't get as much for it."

"Hmm," said Greta. "I have some things my mom was going to give away."

"I do, too," said Samantha.

The next day, Samantha, Greta, and Peter toted their sale items over to Mortimer's house.

"This big table is for you guys," Mortimer told them, pointing to a long folding table. "Wow! You really have a lot of things to sell."

"Is that your table, Mortimer?" asked Peter, pointing to a child's tea table. On it were a chess set and some stuffed animals. "Is it big enough for your stuff?"

"Well, I don't have much," said Mortimer. "In fact that's about all I could find. I hate to get rid of anything."

"I told you!" Samantha rolled her eyes.

"Well, you really take good care of your

things, so why get rid of them?" said Peter. "You never break any of your stuff."

"Your chess set looks almost brand-new," said Greta. "How come you're selling that?"

"Because my uncle gave me another one for Christmas — a really cool one. I never use this set anymore," said Mortimer.

"Ten bucks," said Peter, looking at the price tag on the set. He whistled. "Don't you think that's a little much?"

"Well, the set has all the pieces and the board isn't scratched at all," said Mortimer. "I think it's worth ten dollars." He paused, then started laughing. "If nobody buys it, then I'll just have to keep it."

"I don't care about making money," said Greta. "I just want enough to go to the movies tomorrow!"

The kids unpacked their things and arranged them on the table. Peter had brought some used cleats, an old action hero watch, and some comic books. Greta put out a karate uniform she had out-grown, some jewelry, and a couple of base-ball caps. Samantha arranged a small wire bird cage, some video games, and a box of old toys.

By the time they were set up, several cars had pulled up and people were milling around the tables. A group of kids skidded up on their bikes and checked out the Clue Club kids' tables.

"This is a nice chess set," Phil Platinum told Mortimer. "I have the exact same set, but I'm missing a piece. How much do you want for this one?" He looked at the price tag. "Ten bucks!" he exclaimed. "That's too much. How about five?"

"No way," said Mortimer. "This set is worth more than that."

"That's too much for me," Phil said. He looked over Mortimer's collection of stuffed animals. "How much for this?" he asked, picking up a toy kangaroo.

"Two dollars," said Mortimer. "It even

has a pouch." And he stuck one of his fingers in the pouch to show Phil.

"Okay," said Phil. "That's more like it. My sister collects kangaroos. I'll get it for her. Can you hold it for me? I'll have to go home and get money."

"Sure," said Mortimer.

"Good. I'll come back for it later," said Phil.

"Hey, Mortimer," Peter called out. "Do you have any bags for the things that people buy?"

"Oh, yeah," said Mortimer. "I'll get some." He ran into the house, and a few minutes later he came out with a bunch of plastic bags. "Here you go," he said, handing some to Peter.

Victor Vivid was checking out Mortimer's table when he returned.

"You've got some pretty wild stuffed animals here, Mortimer," Victor said. "I've never seen a stuffed yak before."

"Most yaks are tame, Victor — not wild," Mortimer joked.

"Hey, Phil," said Victor. "There's a chess set just like yours. The pieces are the same and everything."

"Never mind," Phil said. "It's too much. Say, have you got two dollars?"

"Yeah," answered Victor. "Why?"

"Loan it to me. I'll pay you back when I get home," said Phil.

"Okay," said Victor, digging into his pocket for the money.

Phil took the two bills and handed them to Mortimer. "Here," he said, picking up the stuffed kangaroo. "I'll take the kangaroo now."

"I don't think so," said Peter suddenly.

"Why not?" said Phil.

"Because you're taking more than the kangaroo," said Peter.

How does Peter know Phil is taking something else? What is it?

"Since Mortimer's set was too expensive to buy, you decided to take the queen you were missing," said Greta.

"So you stuck the queen in the kangaroo's pouch," finished Samantha. "The kangaroo was something you could afford to buy."

"Phil's plan almost worked," said Mortimer. "But Peter put a checkmate on his move."

36

SOLUTION
The Case of the Chess Caper

"What are you talking about?" said Phil. "You're trying to take part of Mortimer's chess set," said Peter.

"But the chess set is right here," said Mortimer.

"Not the queen," said Greta. She pointed to the square on the board where the queen had been.

"You're right!" shouted Mortimer. "Where is it?"

"It's in the kangaroo," said Samantha. Sure enough, inside the pouch was the missing queen.

"How did you know I took it?" asked Phil.

"I heard Victor say this set was just like yours — the same pieces and everything," said Peter. "So I looked at the pieces and that's when I saw that one of the queens was missing."

The Case of the Dusty Clue

"**C**an I, Mom?" pleaded Mortimer. Mortimer wanted to have this Saturday's Clue Jr. meeting in his clubhouse.

"I think it's fine to have your meeting in the clubhouse," Mrs. Mustard agreed. "But first you'll have to clean it."

"Thanks!" exclaimed Mortimer, running to phone the other club members.

Saturday morning the Clue Club kids came over early to help Mortimer clean the clubhouse. Carrying brooms, buckets, and mops, they peeked inside.

"Oooh." Greta frowned. Everything was covered with a thick layer of dust from the winter.

"Yech," said Mortimer making a face. "We'd better get more sponges."

"Look at all this stuff you left out here,

Mortimer," exclaimed Peter. "There's that old Clue Jr. game we were looking for."

"Hey! Here's my glove!" Mortimer exclaimed, picking up a baseball mitt from the floor. "I thought I'd lost it."

"Wow. Look at the floor where the glove was," said Samantha.

"What's wrong with it?" asked Peter, peering down.

"It's clean!" said Samantha.

"Yeah." Greta laughed. "That's because Mortimer's glove was covering up this spot."

"Hmm," said Peter. He wiped his finger across a bench, then held it up to his face. "Look at this dust. We've got a lot of work to do before we can have our meeting."

"I say we have the meeting in the house and clean this place after lunch," said Mortimer. "It's going to take us a long time to get it clean enough for my parents."

"Good idea!" said Peter. "I had to clean my room before I came over and I've had enough cleaning for now."

"How come you cleaned your room so early in the morning?" asked Samantha.

"I wanted to bring my new video game to the meeting," said Peter. "But I couldn't find it. My mom and dad said it was probably in my room but it was just too messy to find anything in there. So I had to clean my room."

"Did you find the video game?" asked Mortimer.

"Yeah. It was in my room," said Peter as he pulled the hand-held game from his pocket. Everyone laughed.

"No wonder you couldn't find the game," said Greta. "Your room probably looked like the inside of your locker."

"Hey! I cleaned my locker out last month!" Peter exclaimed.

"Yeah, and you found the gloves you lost at Christmas," Mortimer teased.

"Let's go inside and have our meeting," said Samantha. "There's a new mystery book that I want to show you."

Everyone ran back into Mortimer's house

for their meeting. Afterward, they played a few games of Clue Jr. while they ate lunch.

"I see you left all the mops and buckets outside," Mr. Mustard said to Mortimer. "Are you planning to clean out the clubhouse today?"

"Yep. As soon as we finish this game, Dad," said Mortimer.

"Hey, Peter, show me your new video game," said Samantha. "I've never played *Pirate's Treasure.*"

"Sure," Peter said. "I left it in the clubhouse."

When the kids went back out to the clubhouse, the video game wasn't there.

"Peter, you lost your video game again!" giggled Samantha.

"Maybe not," said Mortimer, taking his magnifying glass out of his back pocket. "I think someone has been in the clubhouse since this morning. Look at the footprints." He pointed to the floor.

"I can't tell," said Greta. "There are too many. They all look like ours."

"Let's look around for other clues," said Peter.

"That's a nice hat, Mortimer," said Greta. She pointed to an upside-down baseball cap. "If you're never going to wear it, I will."

"That's not mine," said Mortimer.

"It belongs to Ted Tint," said Samantha, peering at the hat. Ted was a kid who lived down the block from Mortimer.

"Wow! How do you know?" asked Peter.

"Easy," Samantha answered. "He wrote his name on the visor."

"If he's been in the clubhouse, maybe he knows something about my video game," said Peter.

"Let's call him up and have him come over and get his cap," said Greta.

"Good idea!" said Mortimer.

When Ted arrived he looked at the cap. "Yeah, that's mine. I must have left it here last summer when we camped out in your backyard. Remember?"

"Oh, yeah." Mortimer shrugged.

"Look, there's Greg's thermos," Ted said. "And Brad's flashlight. Everybody must have left stuff here from the campout." He picked up his cap. "I'm glad to have this back. I didn't know what happened to it."

Ted put on his cap. "Well, I have to go," he said, looking at the broom and dustpan. "I want to get out of here before you guys start sweeping. I'm allergic to dust."

"It didn't bother you when you were here before," said Samantha.

"Last summer?" said Ted.

"No," said Samantha. "When you were here earlier today."

"I wasn't here today," said Ted.

"Yes, you were," said Samantha. "And I'll bet you took Peter's video game while you were here."

Why does Samantha think Ted took Peter's video game?

SOLUTION
The Case of the Dusty Clue

"Why do you think I took Peter's video game?" said Ted.

Samantha pointed to the place where Ted's cap had been. It was covered with dust. Then she lifted up a magazine that had been sitting in the clubhouse all winter.

"Look," said Peter. "There's a clean space underneath the magazine."

"Just like there was under Mortimer's baseball glove," said Greta.

"But there's no clean spot under your cap," said Samantha.

"That's right," said Mortimer. "If your cap was here all winter, there wouldn't be dust underneath it."

"And the cap would be covered with dust, too," said Greta.

"Where's my video game?" shouted Peter.

"It's at my house," Ted admitted. "I saw you guys in the clubhouse but when I came over you had already gone inside. I just borrowed the game, Peter. I'll go home and get it."

"Well, I guess we cleaned up that mystery," laughed Greta.

The Case of the Mailbox Mystery

After school the Clue Club kids decided to go to Greta's house to do their homework. When they got there, they saw Mrs. Green busy planting flowers along the front of the house. She had already planted flowers in boxes that hung from the front porch railing.

"Are you still planting out here, Mom?" called Greta. "You were doing this yesterday, too."

"And probably tomorrow, as well," Mrs. Green said. "I have more flowers to put on the side of the house. Then I want to put some in the planter around the mailbox." She pointed to the mailbox at the top of the porch stairs, then stood up and dusted off her pants.

"I'm glad everyone came over today,"

she said. "You can all play with these kittens." At her feet were four kittens rolling around in the grass. They belonged to Greta's cat, Mittens. "I can't leave them in the house alone. They're not completely trained yet and they might get on the tables and knock things over. But it's not much different outside. Look!"

The kittens were jumping in and out of the flower boxes and playing with the flowers. Two of them were batting at their reflections in the small puddles of water made when Mrs. Green watered her new plants.

Greta stooped to pick up the mail, which was scattered on the porch beneath the mailbox. "What happened to the mail, Mom?" she asked. "It's all over the porch."

"I don't know, honey," her mother replied. "I didn't notice."

"Maybe Mr. Post was playing basketball with the letters and missed the mailbox," suggested Samantha with a smile.

"Looks like the kittens found them before you did," said Mrs. Green, laughing. She held up an envelope and pointed to a tiny, muddy pawprint on it. The kids laughed.

"You know, the same thing happened yesterday," said Mrs. Green. "The mail was all over the porch. I'll have to ask Mr. Post about that tomorrow when he delivers the mail."

"Hey!" said Peter. "A mystery!"

"Can we help you solve it?" asked Samantha.

"You bet!" said Mrs. Green.

"Maybe it's Howard Hue from down the street," said Greta.

"Why, dear?" her mother asked.

"Because he's mad at me," Greta answered. "I wouldn't let him play with my rabbit last week. He's too rough with Ginger."

"I don't blame you," said Samantha.

"Well, let's see what's happening before we accuse Howard," Mrs. Green said.

The next day, the kids came to Greta's

house again to check on the mail mystery. Once again the mail was on the ground when the kids got there after school. What was more, Mrs. Green had missed Mr. Post that day. She had left her gardening to go inside and answer the phone — just when Mr. Post delivered the mail.

"Listen. Tomorrow we'll be here for our Clue Jr. Club meeting," Greta reminded the others. "We'll watch for Mr. Post. Maybe we can find out what's happening to our mail."

Saturday morning the kids had their Clue meeting outside on Greta's porch. The weather was warm and sunny and they took Mittens and her kittens out with them.

During the meeting, Mrs. Green came onto the porch. "I'm going to run some errands, Greta," she said. "Dad's inside. If you go in, bring the kitties and put the flowerpot here in front of the cat door so they can't get out." She pointed to a large flowerpot to one side of the door, and then to one of the squares in the front door. It was actually a hinged door for Mittens to use to go in and out of the house.

"Okay," said Greta. "See you later, Mom."

After the meeting the kids set up the Clue Jr. board to play a few games. Around noon they saw Mr. Post coming down the block.

"Here we go!" whispered Greta. "Hello, Mr. Post!" she called out.

"Hello there, Greta," Mr. Post answered. "How are you kids today?"

"Fine," they all replied. They watched closely as Mr. Post carefully pushed several letters and a magazine into the mailbox. He noticed all the kids staring at him.

"Anything wrong?" he asked them.

"Oh, no!" Greta said. "Nothing. I'm just expecting a letter from my . . . my cousin."

"I see," said Mr. Post. "Well, I hope it's here today. So long, now."

"So long," they all said together.

"Well?" said Greta.

"Well, nothing!" said Peter. "The letters are in the mailbox."

"Now what?" asked Samantha.

"Let's just play some more Clue Jr. and wait and see," said Mortimer.

"Good idea," said Peter.

After they had played a game, Greta said, "Let's get something to drink while we play."

"Do you have anything to snack on?" asked Mortimer.

"Oh, yeah," Greta said. "Mom made us some sandwiches. We may as well have lunch."

"All right!" said Mortimer. The kids gathered up the kittens and brought them inside. Then Greta led the way into the kitchen, where a plate of sandwiches was waiting.

After the kids finished lunch, they each poured themselves a glass of lemonade and went back outside, where the kittens were frolicking on the porch again.

"Look!" Peter exclaimed. He pointed to where the mail was scattered on the ground again.

"Oh, no!" exclaimed Greta. "It happened again. And we missed it. Now I know it was Howard. He waited until we went inside."

"Well, let's pick up the letters," said Mortimer, taking his magnifying glass out of his pocket. "Maybe we'll find some clues on them."

"I think I know what's happening," said Samantha. "And I think if we put the mail back into the mailbox, who ever did it will push the mail out again."

"You think there's someone else besides Howard?" asked Greta.

"I don't think it's Howard at all," said Samantha.

"What should we do?" asked Peter.

"Just put the mail back in the mailbox

and sit down and wait," Samantha answered.

So the kids put the mail in the mailbox and sat down in the porch chairs to wait.

How does Samantha know the culprits will show? Who are they?

might push something off a table and break it."

"Right," said Samantha. "So each time the mail came she was outside garden- ing — with the kittens! And this time . . ."

Samantha pointed to the flowerpot stand- ing to one side of the door.

"Yikes! I see," said Greta. "I forgot to move the flowerpot in front of the cat door, so the kittens got out while we were eating lunch."

"Yeah," said Mortimer. "And they pushed the letters out of the mailbox."

"At least the letters can't break!" laughed Peter.

SOLUTION
The Case of the Mailbox Mystery

As the kids watched the mailbox, the kittens began climbing all over the porch chairs and the railing. Finally they crawled into the mailbox, where they promptly pushed all the letters out onto the porch.

"The kittens did it!" exclaimed Greta.

"How did you know?" Mortimer asked Samantha.

"Two clues," Samantha answered. "The first was the pawprint on one of the letters."

"But the kittens could have stepped on the letter when it was lying on the porch," said Greta.

"That's true," said Samantha. "But I also noticed that the kittens were always outside when this happened. Remember your mom saying she didn't want to leave them inside while she was gardening?"

"Oh, yeah," said Peter. "Because they

7

The Case of the Broken Roller Skates

Mrs. Scarlet pulled up in front of Mortimer's house and honked the car horn. Mortimer ran out carrying a pair of skates over his shoulder. Samantha had just gotten a new pair of roller skates for Christmas. Since it was too cold to skate outside, Mrs. Scarlet was taking everyone to the roller rink.

Mortimer climbed into the car. "Let me see your new skates, Samantha," he said, buckling his seat belt. "Hey, they're regular roller skates!"

"Yeah," Samantha said. "And my parents had kind of a hard time finding them. Most of the skates now are in-line."

"Why didn't you just get those?" asked Peter. "They go super fast!"

"That's why!" exclaimed Samantha. "I

don't want to go super fast. I just want to go sort of fast."

"Not me," said Greta. "The faster the better."

"Except not at a rink," said Mortimer. "You might bump into some slowpoke," he said looking right at Samantha.

"Here we are," said Mrs. Scarlet. "I'll see you later this afternoon. Have a good time."

Out on the rink, Samantha was practically the only one wearing roller skates. "See what I mean?" said Samantha. "Everyone else has in-line skates."

"It's true," said Peter. "I don't see anyone else wearing roller skates."

"Who cares?" said Greta. "As long as you can skate. Let's go!" She rolled out onto the rink with the others following.

After about an hour of skating, Mortimer called everyone over to the side of the rink. "Anyone else hungry?" he asked.

"I am!" said Peter.

"Me too," said Greta.

"Me three," agreed Samantha. "We can skate some more this afternoon."

The kids left their skates under one of the benches and headed for the food court. After some pizza, they were ready for another turn or two on the rink. But when they sat down on the bench to put on their skates, they found Samantha's new white roller skates all scuffed up.

"Oh, no," she cried. "What happened to my new skates?"

"Wow! They're all dirty," said Mortimer.

"But they were fine before lunch," said Samantha.

"It looks like somebody used them while we were eating," said Peter.

"Looks like they used your gloves, too," said Greta, pulling a glove out of one skate. "And they lost one. There's only one here."

"That's not mine," said Samantha. She pulled out her gloves. "Mine are solid blue. Those are polka-dotted." She put on her skates and stood up. "Now one wheel is loose, too," she said, rolling back and forth on the left skate. Just then, the wheel fell off.

"Oh, great!" Samantha wailed. "My brand-new skates are broken."

"Maybe I can fix it," said Peter. But after trying for a few minutes, Peter shook his head. "It's no use, Samantha. I'm sorry, but I can't fix the wheel."

"That's okay, Peter," said Samantha sadly. "Thanks for trying."

"Why don't you rent some skates for now?" said Mortimer. The kids pooled their money and rented Samantha some in-line skates.

Greta took Samantha's hand and rolled her out onto the rink. "Come on," she said. "I'll help you."

"Me too," said Mortimer grabbing Samantha's other hand.

"And I'll clear the way for you!" said Peter, skating out in front of them.

Going around the turn, a girl was skating so fast that she almost knocked Peter over. "Hey!" he shouted. "Watch out!" The girl's feet went out from under her and she fell down.

"You were going too fast," Greta told the girl as they helped her up.

"Yeah, way too fast for a rink," said Mortimer.

"I know. I'm sorry I ran into you," the girl told Peter.

"Let's go sit down," said Samantha. The kids and the girl skated over to the side and sat down on the bench where they had left their bags and Samantha's skates. The girl introduced herself as Mary Mauve.

"Are you okay?" Mortimer asked Mary.

"Yeah," she answered. "I just don't know how to stop on these in-line skates. I can't even stand up on them very well."

"Sometimes they're hard to get used to," said Peter. "But the first thing you have to learn is how to stop."

"That's just it," Mary exclaimed. "I can't figure out how to use the brakes. I wish I had some plain old roller skates like

yours." She pointed to Samantha's skates. "I can skate well on those."

"Yeah. And you just did skate on them," said Greta.

"What?" said Mary. "What do you mean?"

"I think you used these skates in the rink a little while ago," said Greta.

"Why would I use her skates?" Mary asked. "I have my own."

"You said it yourself," said Greta. "Because they're easier to skate with."

"You can't prove that," Mary said.

"Maybe. Maybe not," said Greta.

Why does Greta think Mary used Samantha's new skates?

SOLUTION
The Case of the Broken Roller Skates

Greta handed Mary the glove she had found in Samantha's skate. "Here. You dropped this."

Mary reached around to her back pocket and discovered that she had only one glove. It was the twin to the glove Greta had given her. "Oh," she said, blushing.

"Greta found the glove in one of Samantha's skates," explained Mortimer. "You must have dropped it when you 'borrowed' her skates."

Mary admitted she had used Samantha's skates that day. After she explained to her father what had happened, Mr. Mauve offered to have Samantha's skates repaired.

"Good," Samantha sighed. "My new skates will be almost new again."

"Yeah, I guess your new skates really did get broken in today," laughed Peter.

8

The Case of the Barking Dog

Mortimer, Samantha, and Greta were on their way to Peter's house. They were having their Saturday Clue Jr. Club meeting there. The night before, it had turned very cold and snowed about three inches. As they reached Peter's, the three kids saw him shoveling his walk. Greta made a snowball and threw it on the sidewalk that Peter had just cleaned.

"Hey!" Peter shouted, turning around. His frown turned to a smile when he saw his three friends. He dropped his shovel and bent down to make a snowball. The other three quickly made more snowballs, and soon they were all having a snowball fight. Afterward, the kids made snow angels and a huge snowman, then they helped Peter finish shoveling.

When they finally piled into Peter's house, Mortimer's eyeglasses fogged up. "Oooh, I hate it when that happens," he said. He pulled off his glasses and began cleaning them.

"What happened?" asked Greta.

"My glasses were cold from being outside so long," said Mortimer. "Then when I walked into Peter's warm house the heat made them steam up."

"That always happens if you stay out in the cold for very long," said Samantha.

"Let's hurry up and start the meeting," said Peter. "I have some good news."

"Cool!" said Greta, pulling off her gloves. Everyone took off their boots and scarves and hung up their coats and hats.

"Here," Mr. Plum said, setting some steaming cups on the dining room table. "This will warm you up!" He had made hot chocolate for the kids to drink during their meeting.

"Thanks!" exclaimed the four cold children.

As president of the Clue Jr. Club, Peter called the meeting to order. After Samantha, the secretary, read the minutes from the last meeting, Peter called for new news. Then he raised his hand in the air before anyone else could say a word.

"I have some great new news," he said excitedly. "I shoveled off Mrs. Goodview's sidewalk this morning and she wants to have another Mystery Movie Club this year."

"Great!" shouted Greta.

"She's going to start showing mystery movies every Friday night in January," Peter said."

"Cool!" said Mortimer.

"Wait, Mortimer. I didn't tell you the best part." Peter laughed. "Mrs. Goodview wants us to help her choose the movies!"

"Yes!" said Mortimer. "Let's make a list right now!"

"How about *Mystery at Rodeo Ranch* for starters?" said Samantha.

"That's a great movie!" said Peter. "Secretary Scarlet, will you write down the list?"

"Sure, President Plum," giggled Samantha.

"*The Circus Clown Caper* is a good one," said Mortimer.

"Let's put that at the bottom of the list," said Greta. "Maybe it's a good movie, but I hate clowns."

Soon Samantha had a list of fifteen movies to show Mrs. Goodview.

"Any more news?" asked Peter.

"I'm getting hungry," said Mortimer. "Isn't it about time to eat?"

"That's definitely old news, Mortimer!" Peter kidded him. "You're always hungry!"

"I second the motion," said Greta. Everyone headed for the kitchen and some lunch.

"Peter, would you let Bosco out in the backyard for a few minutes?" Mrs. Plum called up from the basement.

"Sure, Mom," said Peter. "Here, Bosco!

Here, boy!" When Bosco bounded into the kitchen, Peter opened the back door and let him out into the backyard.

"No matter how bad the weather is, Bosco always wants to go out," Peter said, shaking his head.

As the kids began eating their sandwiches, they heard Bosco barking. "I'll bet Bosco's a good watchdog," said Greta.

"Yeah. He always barks when something's going on outside," said Peter.

For the next five minutes Bosco barked off and on. Suddenly he began yelping loudly. Mr. Plum hurried to the door with the kids right behind him. From the porch they could see Darryl Dye running toward the back gate.

"Stop!" yelled Mr. Plum. "Get over here, young man!" Darryl froze, then turned around.

"What do you think you're doing?" Mr. Plum asked angrily.

"I saw these kids throwing snowballs

at your dog. I just chased them off," said Darryl.

"Well, then, come in the house and tell us who you saw," said Mr. Plum.

Darryl stamped the snow off his boots and came in the back door. "So what happened?" Mr. Plum asked him.

"Well, I was next door playing video games with Eric," Darryl said. "I just walked out the door to go home. I heard the dog barking and I saw a couple of kids throwing snowballs at him. So I ran over and made them stop."

"Do you know who they were?" asked Mr. Plum.

"No," said Darryl.

"I do," said Mortimer. "At least I know who one of them was."

"Did you see him?" asked Darryl.

"No, but I bet it was you," said Mortimer.

Why does Mortimer think Darryl was throwing snowballs at Bosco?

SOLUTION
The Case of the Barking Dog

"Me?" cried Darryl. "That's the thanks I get for trying to help Peter's dog?"

"I think you were lying about Bosco," said Mortimer.

"Then prove it," said Darryl.

"Okay," said Mortimer. "The proof is that you can't see very well."

"My glasses are steamed up," said Darryl. "That's all."

"But that only happens if you've been outside for a while," said Peter.

"That's right. You said you had just come out of Eric's house," said Samantha. "But if that was true, your glasses wouldn't have steamed up."

"You must have been outside long enough for your glasses to get good and cold," said Greta.

"What's your story, Darryl?" said Mr.

Plum sternly. "We can always go next door and ask Eric when you left."

Darryl looked down at his feet and admitted to throwing snowballs at Bosco.

"You picked up on an important clue when Darryl's cold glasses fogged up, Mortimer," said Samantha.

"Yeah," said Mortimer, waving his own glasses in the air. "Even without my glasses I could see that clue right away."